TIMELESS CLASSICS

THE ADVENTURES OF
HUCKLEBERRY FINN

Mark Twain

– ADAPTED BY –
Joanne Suter

SADDLEBACK
EDUCATIONAL PUBLISHING

TIMELESS CLASSICS

Literature Set 1 (1719-1844)

A Christmas Carol
The Count of Monte Cristo
Frankenstein
Gulliver's Travels
The Hunchback of Notre Dame
The Last of the Mohicans

Oliver Twist
Pride and Prejudice
Robinson Crusoe
The Swiss Family Robinson
The Three Musketeers

Literature Set 2 (1845-1884)

The Adventures of Huckleberry Finn
The Adventures of Tom Sawyer
Around the World in 80 Days
Great Expectations
Jane Eyre
The Man in the Iron Mask

Moby Dick
The Prince and the Pauper
The Scarlet Letter
A Tale of Two Cities
20,000 Leagues Under the Sea

Literature Set 3 (1886-1908)

The Call of the Wild
Captains Courageous
Dracula
Dr. Jekyll and Mr. Hyde
The Hound of the Baskervilles
The Jungle Book

Kidnapped
The Red Badge of Courage
The Time Machine
Treasure Island
The War of the Worlds
White Fang

SADDLEBACK
EDUCATIONAL PUBLISHING
www.sdlback.com

ISBN: 978-1-61651-068-8
eBook: 978-1-60291-802-3

Printed in Malaysia

23 22 21 20 19   9 10 11 12 13

TIMELESS CLASSICS

Contents

1 I Join the Robber Gang 5

2 I Fool Pap and Get Away............................. 11

3 Me and Jim Run Off................................... 16

4 The Snakeskin Does Its Work 23

5 The Grangerfords Take Me In...................... 30

6 The Duke and the King 37

7 I Trick the Rapscallions 43

8 I Have a New Name 51

9 Trying to Help Jim 58

10 Why They Don't Hang Jim 66

11 Nothing More to Write............................... 74

Activities 78

| 1 |

I Join the Robber Gang

I'm Huck Finn. You don't know about me unless you read *The Adventures of Tom Sawyer*. That book was made by Mr. Mark Twain. He told the truth, mainly. Well, there might have been a few things he stretched. But that's O.K. Seems like everybody stretches the truth sometime—except maybe Tom's Aunt Polly or the Widow Douglas. They're in the book, too.

Now, that book about Tom Sawyer ended just when Tom and me got rich. We found some robbers' gold hidden in a cave. We got $6,000 each! Judge Thatcher, he kept the money for us. He gives it out to us a dollar a day, all year round. Why, that's more money than a fellow knows what to do with!

After that, the Widow Douglas took me in to live with her. Her sister, Miss Watson, lives there, too. They're both bent on civilizing me—giving me manners and religion and such. I ran away once. But Tom Sawyer hunted me up. He said I could be in his robber band—but only if I went back to the widow's.

The widow read to me from the Bible. She meant well, but those stories are about dead people. Truth is, I don't much care about dead people. Miss Watson was even worse. "Don't put your feet up there, Huckleberry Finn!" she'd say. She'd frown at me over her goggles, and sometimes she'd call me wicked. It all made me tired.

One night after Miss Watson had been pecking at me, I went up to my room. I sat there so lonesome I almost wished I was dead. Then a spider crawled up my arm, so I flipped it off. It landed in a candle and burned up! I don't need to tell you, that was an awful sign. It was bound to bring me bad luck.

I sat there shivering, thinking about the bad luck that was coming. Then I heard a sound from out in the trees.

"Me-yow! Me-yow!"

I recognized Tom's call right away. So I scrambled out the window and slid to the ground. Sure enough, there was Tom Sawyer waiting for me.

Tom and me headed out of the garden. As we passed the kitchen, I tripped over a tree root. We dropped and laid still. Miss Watson's slave Jim was sitting in the kitchen doorway. He got up and stretched his big bones. Then he calls out, "Who there? I hears something! Huh! I'm just gonna sit right down 'til I hears it again." We stayed quiet until Jim began to snore.

Then Tom went into the kitchen to get us some candles. He left five cents on the table for pay. I wanted to sneak off right away, but not Tom! He had to play a trick on Jim first. He slipped Jim's hat off and hung it up in a tree.

When Jim woke up in the morning, he told everyone that some witches had come in the night. "They set me under the trees and hung my hat on a limb. Look! They left me this five-cent piece!" The other slaves laughed some at Jim's story. But they wouldn't touch that five-cent piece. They thought the devil had put his hands on it.

Well, anyway, me and Tom went on our way that night. We met up with some of the boys and took an old boat down the river a mile or two. First Tom made everybody swear to keep a secret. Then he showed us a cave in the hill. We lit candles and crawled in.

"Now, we'll start this band of robbers," Tom says proudly. "We'll call it Tom Sawyer's Gang."

Everybody had to swear an oath. Tom had gotten the idea out of some pirate book. We swore to kill the families of anyone who told the gang's secrets.

Then someone says, "What about Huck Finn? He ain't got no family. His ol' drunk father ain't been seen around here in years."

I wanted to join the gang real bad, so I offered them Miss Watson. When I said they could kill *her* if I talked, they agreed!

We all stuck a pin in our fingers to get some blood. Then we made a mark on a paper. We wrote our names on the cave wall in blood, too.

We elected Tom the first captain of our robber band. Then we started home.

I climbed into my window at daybreak.

The new clothes the widow had got me was all dirty with clay. I was dog-tired.

Next morning when Miss Watson saw my clothes, I was in big trouble! The widow, she just looked sorry and sad. Then Miss Watson took me in the closet and prayed.

Once I tried praying for what I wanted, but it didn't work. I got a fishline, but no hooks. That line weren't no good to me without hooks!

I hadn't seen my Pap for more than a year now. That was fine with me. He used to always be after me. Any time he could get his hands on me, he'd let me have it. Well, about this time they found a drowned body floating on its back in the river. They said it looked like my Pap, all ragged and long-haired. But I knowed that a drowned man don't float on his back, but on his face. It was probably a woman dressed up in a man's clothes. So I still worried that old Pap would turn up by and by. I wished he wouldn't.

Me and the gang, we played robber for about a month. Then the gang broke up. We hadn't robbed nobody. We hadn't killed no people, either. We just pretended.

One time Tom Sawyer says we should attack

this Sunday school picnic. He tells us those little kids we see running around are *really* soldiers on elephants and camels. He says that magicians are making them look like Sunday school kids. Then he tells me that those magicians got magic lamps. They just rub a lamp and a bunch of genies comes out and does stuff for them!

Well, I found me an old lamp after dinner one night. I rubbed and rubbed—but no genies came out! So I judged that the whole story was just one of Tom Sawyer's lies. I reckon maybe *Tom* could see magicians and genies. But me, I just saw a Sunday school picnic.

It weren't long after that I lit the candle in my bedroom. There was Pap sitting on the bed. He was waiting for me.

| 2 |

I Fool Pap
and Get Away

I reckon I was pretty scared to see Pap. His hair was long, hanging down like dirty old vines. His clothes were rags. His boots were so busted that his toes stuck through. I stood there looking at him. He sat there looking at me.

By and by, he says, "Fine clothes you got. Ain't you a high and mighty fellow?"

"Maybe I am, maybe I ain't," I says.

"Don't you give me no lip. They say you can read and write. You think you're better than your father now, don't you? Who put you up to that foolishness?"

"The widow. She taught me."

"Well, I'll learn her not to meddle. You drop that school, you hear? Your poor dead mother, she couldn't read or write neither.

Let me hear ya read something."

I took up a book and began reading. It was a story about George Washington. Pap whacked the book across the room.

"It's so!" he says. "You *can* do it! If I catch you at that school again, I'll tan you good. I heard about you being rich, too. That's why I come. You get me that money."

"It's a lie," I says. "You can ask Judge Thatcher. He'll tell you I ain't got no money." That was the truth. I had nothing. It was all put away in the bank.

"Oh, I'll ask him, all right," says Pap. "I'll make him tell me, too. Hey, you got anything in your pocket?"

"Just a dollar," I says, "and that's for—"

Pap took it to buy some whiskey. Then he said he'd lick me good if I didn't drop out of school right quick.

Next day Pap went to Judge Thatcher. He tried to bully him into giving him my money. He sweared he'd get the law on his side.

Judge Thatcher and Widow Douglas went to the court. They tried to take me away from Pap. But a new judge was there who didn't know the old man. He said Pap should get another chance at me.

That judge found out about Pap soon enough. Old Pap got drunk and fell off a porch. He broke his arm in two places.

As soon as Pap's arm got better, he was after me again. When he saw me going to school, he chased me. I really didn't care about school that much before. But now I reckoned I'd go just to spite Pap.

But Pap waited for me one spring day. He catched me and took me upriver to an old log hut in the woods. He kept me locked up, and I never got a chance to run off.

After a while I got used to the lazy life. I sort of liked it—except when Pap got drunk and went after me.

By and by Pap got too handy with the stick. One time he almost killed me. And he got to locking me in too much. Once he was gone three days. I was dreadful lonesome. It was then I made up my mind to get away.

I found an old saw and hid it in the hut. Next time Pap locked me in, I went to work. I sawed a hole in the wall. Then I filled up a canoe with stuff I'd need—some food and fishlines and matches. I fetched a gun.

Then I went back to the cabin. I smashed the door with an axe, just like robbers might do it. I killed a pig and laid him on the ground to bleed. Then I dragged a sack of rocks down to the river. I left plenty of marks so people would think those robbers had drug my body there and throwed it in.

After that, I pulled out some of my hair and stuck it on the axe. I carried the pig off so no one could find him. All the while I'm wishing Tom

Sawyer was with me. I knowed he would take an interest in this business. He'd probably throw in some fancy touches.

I climbed in the canoe and paddled out to Jackson's Island. Then I hid the canoe and laid down in the woods for a nap.

The sound of a cannon boom woke me up. I sneaked to the shore and hid behind a log. A ferryboat came drifting along. Most everybody was on that boat. There was Pap and Judge Thatcher and Tom Sawyer. They was so close, I could hear them talking about my murder. The cannon boomed again. Everybody knows that cannon booms is supposed to bring up bodies. I watched the ferry drift by, booming now and then. Once it passed out of sight, I knowed I was all right. Nobody else would be hunting for me.

I felt about ready for another nap. But back in the woods, what should I run right into but a campfire. There lay a man rolled up in a blanket! I watched him close, and pretty soon he moved. My heart jumped.

| 3 |

Me and Jim
Run Off

The man by the fire sat up. It was Miss Watson's Jim!

"Hello, Jim!" I shouted out.

Jim stared at me wild-eyed. "Mercy! It's Huck's ghost!" he cries. "Go on now. Get back in that river where you belong!"

Well, I soon made Jim understand that I wasn't no ghost. I was tired of being lonesome and mighty glad to see him. I told him how I faked my own killing. He said I must be real smart. He said Tom Sawyer couldn't have done no better.

"What are you doing out here, Jim?" I asked him.

All of a sudden he looked uneasy. "Huck," he says, "I— I done run off."

"*Jim!*"

"You won't tell on me, will you Huck?"

"I won't, Jim. Honest, I won't! Folks might call me a low-down Abolitionist. They might hate me for keeping quiet. But I swear I ain't a-going to tell."

"Why, I *had* to run, Huck! I heard ol' Miss Watson talking to a slave trader. She was going to sell me down to New Orleans for $800.00! I heard the widow tell her not to do it, then I didn't wait to hear no more. I got out of there mighty quick."

Some birds flew over just then. Jim said that meant it was going to rain. He told me about all kinds of signs. He said you shouldn't count the things you cook for dinner. That would bring bad luck. He said it was bad luck to shake a tablecloth after sundown. Seemed to me like all the signs Jim knew brought bad luck.

Then we got to talking about getting rich. "I'm rich now," says Jim. "I owns myself—and I'm worth $800.00!"

Those birds had been right. Shortly, it began to rain. Jim showed me a cave he'd found, and we settled in. We could hear the thunder rumblin' and grumblin' outside.

"It's right nice in here," I says. "I wouldn't want to be nowhere else."

The rain kept up. For 10 or 12 days, the river rose. When the storm stopped, we paddled around the island in the canoe. One night we spied a raft floating on the river. We pulled it in to shore and hid it good in a thick stand of trees.

Another night, here comes a *house* floating along! We paddled out and got aboard. It was just getting light out, so we peeked in one of the windows. First thing we saw was something laying on the floor. It looked like a *man*!

"Hello, you!" Jim hollers.

It didn't move.

"That man ain't asleep, Huck," says Jim. "He's dead!"

Jim went in. He bent down and looked. "It's a dead man, all right. I reckon he been dead two or three days. Come in, Huck—but don't look at him. You don't need to see no dead man."

Jim threw some old rags over him, but he

didn't need to. I didn't want to see him.

There were cards on the floor and some whiskey bottles, too. Men's and women's clothes were piled up. We gathered up some things. We took a tin lantern, some sewing stuff, a quilt, and a fishline.

Then we loaded our haul in the canoe and shoved off. It was daylight, so I made Jim lay down under a quilt so no one would see him. We got home safe.

Back on the island, I wanted to talk about the dead man. Jim said it was bad luck. We looked through the clothes from the dead man's house. There was eight dollars in a coat pocket!

"Hey, Jim," I says. "Remember when I touched that old snakeskin we found the other day? You said I would bring us bad luck. Well, here's eight dollars. I wish we could have bad luck like this every day!"

"Oh, trouble's a-coming," said Jim. He shook his head. "It's a-coming for sure."

The bad luck did come, too. A few days later I killed a rattlesnake. For a joke, I curled it up by Jim's blanket. I was thinking how I'd laugh when he spied it. Well, when Jim laid down that night, he landed on top of the snake's mate. That darned ol' snake bit him right on the heel!

Jim was laid up for four days and nights. I swore I would never touch a snakeskin again, now that I seen what come of it.

Days went by, and the river went down. Things was getting kind of slow and dull. That's when I decided to row over to town and see what was going on.

Jim had an idea. He said why didn't I dress up like a girl. That way no one would know me.

It was a good idea. I got into the clothes we had found in the house. I put on a sun-bonnet. All day I practiced getting the hang of being a girl. Just after dark I paddled up to the Illinois shore.

I tied up the canoe at the town dock. There was a light burning in an old shack. No one had lived there for a long time, and I wondered who was staying there now. I sneaked up and peeped in the window.

There sat a woman about 40 years old. She was knitting by a candle. I didn't know her.

That was lucky. If she was a newcomer, she wouldn't know me either. I told myself to talk like a girl. Then I knocked at the door.

"Come in," says the woman. So I did.

"What might your name be?" she asks.

"Sarah Williams. I've walked a long way, and I'm all tired out. My mother is sick, and I've come to get my uncle. He lives at the other end of town."

"Well, you can rest up here," says the woman. "When my husband gets home, he'll walk you the rest of the way."

She got to talking. I just let her clatter along. Pretty soon she starts to tell me about the murder of Huck Finn.

"Some think old Finn done it. Others, they think it was done by a runaway slave named Jim. That fellow run off the very night poor Huck Finn was killed. There's a reward out for him—$300.00. And there's a reward out for Huck Finn's pappy, too—$200.00."

I started to say how Jim didn't kill nobody. But I stopped before I gave myself away. Then the woman tells me how she saw smoke over on Jackson's Island. She says like as not that slave is hiding there. Her husband means to go over and find out.

I got uneasy and couldn't hold still. The woman started looking close at me.

"What did you say your name was, honey?"

"M-Mary Williams." I tried to keep my voice high, but I knew it sounded funny.

"All right now," says the lady, "what's your *real* name? Is it Bill? Or Tom? Or Bob?"

I knew it was no use. "It's George Peters, ma'am," I says. "My family sent me to work for a mean old farmer. I ran away. I got to get going now—before he comes after me."

"Bless you, then, Sarah Mary Williams George Peters," says the lady. "Get on your way—and good luck!"

I got out of there while I could. I headed back to the canoe fast. When I landed on the island, Jim was sound asleep.

"Get up, Jim!" I hollered. "There ain't a minute to lose. They're *after* us!"

| 4 |
The Snakeskin
Does Its Work

I could tell Jim was real scared. You remember that old raft we found? Well, we pulled it out of its hiding place. We loaded on everything we had and tied the canoe behind. Then we shoved out and floated past the foot of the island.

At the first light of day, we tied up and hid in a cove. All day we laid there watching rafts and steamboats head down along the Missouri shore.

When night came, we felt safer. Jim built us a tent on the raft. He laid a dirt floor and made a place for a fire. We fixed up a forked stick to hold a lantern. If we saw a steamboat coming, we'd hang a light to keep from getting run over.

From then on, we traveled at night and hid by day. The fifth night out, we passed the bright lights of St. Louis. It was like the whole world was lit up!

Early each night I'd go ashore. I'd buy a little meal or bacon or other stuff to eat. Sometimes I'd slip into fields and borrow some corn. Pap always said there was no harm in borrowing if you meant to pay them back sometime. The widow said it weren't anything but a soft name for stealing. Me and Jim shot a water-bird now and then. We lived good, drifting down the river, laying on our backs looking up at the stars.

We figured that three more nights would get us to Cairo. The town sits at the bottom of Illinois, where the Ohio River comes in. We would sell the raft. Then we'd take a steamboat way up the Ohio amongst the free states. They didn't have no slaves up that-a-way, so we'd be out of trouble.

The second night, a fog come in. We knew we'd better tie up. I got in the canoe and paddled ahead of the raft. I got the tow-line tied to a little tree on the bank. But just then the current picked up. The raft came booming down the river. It tore the tree out by the roots, and shot on by me! Jim and the raft disappeared in the fog. I jumped in the canoe and paddled after it.

Floating along, I couldn't tell if I was going straight or round in circles. I figured there was nothing more to do until the fog cleared. I laid down in the canoe for a nap.

When I woke up, the stars was out. The fog was gone, so I looked around. I saw a speck up ahead—it was the raft!

Jim was just setting there, sound asleep.

I tied the canoe to the raft and climbed aboard. Then I laid down right under Jim's nose. I pretended I had just waked up.

"Hello, Jim. Have I been asleep?"

"Is that you, Huck? You ain't drowned? You's *back*, Huck! Thank goodness!"

"What are you talking about, Jim?" I says in a sleepy voice.

"Huck Finn, you know you been lost!"

"You must have been dreaming, Jim," I says, having fun with my joke.

Jim looked around. He saw the dirt and leaves that had washed aboard the raft. He saw an oar he'd busted in the fog. Then he looked at me cold-like. Without smiling, he said, "You think you can make a fool of old Jim with a lie. See all that trash washed up on the raft? Well, trash is what *people* is that make a fool of a friend!"

Then Jim went inside the tent. I swore I'd never do no more mean tricks on him. Why, I wouldn't have done that one if I'd knowed it would make him feel that way.

The night clouded up and got hot. I told Jim I was sorry. Then we talked about Cairo and got to worrying. Maybe we'd passed it by in the fog. If we missed Cairo, we'd be back in slave country again. Jim said if he ever got to a free state he'd start saving up money. He'd buy his wife and two children away from their masters.

By and by, we saw a light.

"That's Cairo!" sings out Jim. "I just knows it!"

"I'll take the canoe and go see, Jim."

"Pretty soon I'll be a free man. And I'll say it's all because of Huck Finn! You're my best friend, Huck!"

I got in the canoe and headed toward shore.

I was feeling kind of bad and mixed up. Maybe I done wrong to help Jim run off. After all, helping a slave get free was sort of like stealing somebody's property. The whole thing got to bothering me, and I didn't know what to think. But just then a boat come along. Two men with guns were aboard.

"We're looking for five slaves that run off last night," says one man. "I see a man out there on your raft. Is he black or white?"

"He's white."

"I reckon we'll go see for ourselves," says the man.

"I wish you would," says I. "It's Pap that's there. He's sick—and so is Ma and Mary Ann. I'd be grateful for your help. Everybody goes away when I ask them."

"Say," asks the man, "what's the matter with your family?"

"It's the. . . well, it ain't nothing much."

The man looked scared. "Your pap's got the *smallpox*, don't he? Keep away, boy! We won't go near him. Look, I'll put a $20.00 gold piece on this board. I'll float it over to you. I feel mighty mean leaving you—but

we can't fool with smallpox."

Then the other man lays another $20.00 gold piece on the board.

I took the money and started back to the raft. I'd gone and helped Jim get away again! I figured I should feel bad. But I knew I'd feel a whole lot worse if I'd a turned him in! I just gave up then. I reckoned I wouldn't bother about it no more.

I tied up the canoe and climbed back into the raft. I'll be darned if Jim wasn't gone!

Then I saw his head sticking out of the water.

"Here I is, Huck! I was ready to swim for it if those fellows came. I heard you talking. Darned if you didn't fool 'em! You saved ol' Jim, and I'll never forget it!"

That night we saw more lights. I paddled the canoe toward shore again.

"Mister," I called to a big fellow on the docks. "Is this town Cairo?"

He hollered no and pointed upriver. Then I was *sure* that we'd passed Cairo in the fog.

When I told Jim, he didn't say much. We both knew it was more bad luck from touching that snakeskin.

Then a steamboat came pounding up the river. We lit the lantern so we'd be seen.

All of a sudden we heard bells a-ringing. Someone on board was yelling. Jim went over one side. I went over the other. The steamboat smashed into the raft!

I dove for the bottom. When I came up, I sang out for Jim. I didn't get an answer.

| 5 |

The Grangerfords
Take Me In

When I couldn't find Jim, I swam for shore. I made it safe to the bank and started walking down a road. Before long I came across a big, old-fashioned house. A pack of dogs started barking at me.

"Who's prowling around out there?" a man called out a window.

I says, "It's me—George Jackson, sir."

"What do you want?"

"I don't want nothing, sir. I was just passing by. You see, I fell off the steamboat. I'm only a boy, sir."

"Look here," says the man, "if you're telling the truth, you don't need to be afraid. Stand right where you are. Bob, Tom—you fetch your guns and take a look."

I heard people stirring in the house. Then I see a light through the window.

"Say, George Jackson, do you know the Shepherdsons?"

"No, sir. I never heard of them."

"Step forward, then, George Jackson. Come slow and push the door open."

I went into the house and saw a candle on the floor. There were three men, a sweet-looking gray-haired lady, and two young women. They were all staring at me.

The oldest man held up the candle. He looked me up and down and says, "He ain't no Shepherdson."

Then the old lady began worrying that I was wet. "Buck!" she called.

Buck came downstairs a-rubbing his eyes as if he'd been asleep. He was dragging a gun after him. He looked about as old as me—13 or 14.

Buck led me upstairs. He gave me one of his shirts and some pants to wear.

This family—the Grangerfords—was mighty nice. They had a mighty nice house too. The door had a brass knob. And the table had a cloth with a red and blue eagle painted on it. They ate good food and must have owned a hundred slaves or more.

I told the Grangerfords that my whole family had died. I said I was headed up the river on that steamboat to start a new life. That's when I accidentally fell overboard—and that's how I came to be at their door. They kindly said I could have a home with them as long as I wanted.

I slept in Buck's room. When I waked up on that first morning, darned if I hadn't forgot the name I gave myself. I laid there thinking. When Buck waked up I says, "Buck, can you spell?"

"Yes," he says.

"I bet you can't spell my name," says I. "I dare you to try."

Thinking on it a minute or so, he spells, "G-e-o-r-g-e J-a-x-o-n. There now!"

"Well, you did it!" I says. Later that day I made sure to write it down. I wouldn't want to forget my name again!

There were a *lot* of Grangerfords. They were all fine, good-looking people. The men were tall with broad shoulders and black hair and eyes. The women were beautiful—especially Miss Sophia. She was 20 and gentle like a dove.

Each person had a slave to wait on them. They gave me a slave, too. His name was Jack. Jack had an easy time of it. I wasn't used to having anybody do anything for me.

There used to be more Grangerfords, Buck told me. Some had gotten themselves killed by the Shepherdsons.

There was always a lot of talk about killing and a lot of talk about Shepherdsons. I was wondering why the Grangerford men always carried guns.

Buck explained it all to me. Seems there was another rich family around here. They was the Shepherdsons. About 30 years ago some trouble started. Buck didn't know just what the trouble was or how the shooting started, but it did.

"Turned into a real feud," Buck says.

"Feud?" I says. "What's a feud?"

"It all goes back to the old trouble. Every now and again we kills one of them or they kills one of us. By and by I guess *everybody* will be killed off one way or another. Then there won't be no more feud."

"Those Shepherdsons must be real cowards," I says.

"Nope," says Buck. "There ain't a coward among the Grangerfords nor the Shepherdsons either."

One day I was wandering down to the river, just to be by myself. I saw my slave Jack following after me.

"Master George," he calls. "If you come down to the swamp with me, I got something for you to see."

Jack led me deep into the swamp. We came to a flat little piece of dry land. It was thick with trees and bushes and vines. I started into the place. When I turned around, Jack was gone.

I poked around through the bushes a bit. What do I find but a man laying on the ground asleep. By gosh, it was my old Jim!

Jim told me how he'd swum to shore behind me. He'd been afraid to call out. He didn't want nobody to pick him up and make him a slave again.

"I been patching up the raft," says Jim.

"Is that a fact, Jim? You mean our old raft wasn't smashed all to bits?"

"No, she weren't. She was pretty tore up, and the canoe's gone. But she's all fixed up as good as new. Jack, he found me. He helped me patch up the raft and brought me supplies. We is all set to head out, Huck, whenever you is ready."

I went back to the Grangerfords' to sleep that night. When I waked up in the morning, the place was real quiet. I looked across the room. Buck was already gone.

I got up and wandered downstairs. Every room was just as still as a mouse. Then I come across Jack.

"What's going on?" I says.

"Oh, Master George!" he says, "Miss Sophia's gone! She run off with that young Harney Shepherdson. The family found out and went for their guns. I reckon there'll be some rough times now."

I took off up the river road, looking for Buck. By and by I heard gunfire. I climbed up a cottonwood tree to get a view.

I could see some men on horses and others behind a woodpile. And I could see Buck. Every one of them had a gun! They was a-shooting at each other—*bang, bang, bang!* I could hear their voices shouting, "Kill 'em, kill 'em all!"

The things I saw made me sick. I almost fell out of the tree. I ain't a-going to tell all that happened. It would make me sick again if I was to do that. I wished I hadn't ever come ashore that night to see such things.

I stayed in the tree until it begun to get dark. Then I got down and crept along the riverbank. I saw Buck lying dead by the edge of the water. That made me cry a little. He had been mighty good to me.

Then I ran to find Jim. I wanted to get back on the river.

I never felt easy until we was out in the middle of the Mississippi. I was glad to get away from the feud. Jim was glad to be free of the swamp, too. We both said there weren't no home like a raft, after all. Other places always seem so cramped up. You feel mighty free and easy on a raft.

| 6 |

The Duke and the King

Two or three smooth and lovely days went by. Sometimes we'd have the whole monstrous river to ourselves. Sometimes we'd see a raft or a scow or a steamboat. Maybe we could hear a fiddle or a song coming from one of them crafts. Yep, it's a fine thing to live on a raft. We used to lay on our backs and look up at the sky, all speckled with stars. We'd talk about whether them stars was made or just happened.

One morning I found a canoe. I paddled it up a creek to look for some berries.

All of a sudden, a couple of men come running up a path along the creek. I feared I was a goner. They were sure to be looking for Jim or me!

But then they started begging me to save their lives! They said they was being chased and hadn't done nothing at all.

I could hear dogs and men a-coming after them. So, I let them aboard and lit out. We got back to the raft and stayed hid in a cove.

One of the fellows was about 70. He had a bald head and gray whiskers. He wore a long-tailed coat with big brass buttons. The other fellow was about 30. He was dressed ragged, too. Both of them carried fat, ratty-looking carpetbags.

"What got *you* in trouble?" says the bald-headed fellow to the younger one.

"I'd been selling something that cleans the

dirt off teeth. Problem is, it takes the enamel off, too. I was just sliding out of town when I ran across you. That's my story. What's yours?"

"Well," says the bald-headed man, "I was running a little temperance revival. I was taking in five or six dollars a night speaking on the evils of drink. The townsfolk loved me—especially the women. But word got out that I had a whiskey jug of my own hidden away. Then I heard they was planning to tar and feather me! Seemed like it was about time to move on."

"Old man," says the younger one, "I think we might team up."

"Don't mind if we do," says the bald head. "Where you from?"

The younger fellow sighs as if he's about to cry. "Gentlemen," he says, "I am the Duke of Bridgewater. Here I am," the fellow goes on, "come down from my high place in life. I'm sunk to the company of crooks on a raft."

Jim and I felt sorry for him after that. We agreed to call him "My Lord," and "Your Grace," to make him feel better.

The old man stays quiet a while. Later in the day he pipes up. "There's more than one person on this raft that comes from a high place," he says. Then, by gosh, he begins to cry. "I am a *king*! Yes—you see before you the rightful King of France."

You can bet me and Jim stared then. For a while, we felt sorry for him, too. We took to calling him "Your Majesty" and waiting on him at meals.

It didn't take me long to make up my mind that these two weren't no kings nor dukes at all. They was just liars. I never let on, though. I didn't learn much from Pap. But I did learn the best way to get along with his kind of people. You best let them have their own way—or pretend to.

The Duke and the King asked why we only ran at night. They also asked if Jim was a runaway.

"Goodness, no!" I says. "My Pap just died. All he left me was $16.00, this raft, and his slave, Jim. I aim to take Jim down to my Uncle Ben's farm, south of New Orleans. But people keep trying to take him from me. If I just run at night, they leave me alone."

The Duke had a plan so we could run in

the daytime. He made a sign saying Jim was a runaway slave. Then he got out a rope. "When we see someone coming, we can tie Jim hand and foot," he says. "We'll say we're taking him in."

I thought the Duke was pretty smart. But Jim wasn't happy. He said he hoped we didn't meet any more kings on our trip.

Then the Duke and the King came up with another idea. They decided to put on a play called *Romeo and Juliet*.

The first town we came to, the Duke and the King sold tickets. They set up for the show. The King, he aimed to play the part of Juliet. But when he came on stage, some people threw rocks and rotten apples at him! The Duke said we better get out fast, so we took off running.

At the next town, the Duke and the King tried another show. To make sure they got a good audience, they wrote a sign. It said "Ladies and children not allowed." Pretty near every man in town bought himself a ticket.

We had a full house. But before the show began, the Duke and the King decided we should run for it. We took the ticket money and hightailed it to the raft. Soon we was gliding downstream again.

Them two took in $465.00. I ain't never seen money hauled in like that in my whole life!

By and by the Duke and the King was asleep and snoring. Jim says to me, "Them two is regular *rapscallions*, that's what they is. I don't want no more of 'em, Huck!"

"It's the way I feel, too, Jim. But we've got them on our hands."

I drifted off to sleep then. When I waked up, Jim was sitting with his head down, moaning to himself. I knew he was thinking about his wife and children. Jim was a mighty good fellow, he was.

| 7 |

I Trick the Rapscallions

One day the King and I was in a town getting supplies. We heard that a fellow named Peter Wilks had died. He had left three daughters all alone.

Seems that this Wilks fellow had two brothers who lived way off in England. They were due to arrive any day now to take care of the daughters.

Well, the King started asking lots of questions. Before long we knew all about Peter Wilks and his brothers, Harvey and William. It wasn't hard to guess the King was hatching an idea.

I was right. Later that day the King told the Duke about dead Peter Wilks. He said they should play like they was his brothers.

Right away the King and the Duke started practicing to talk like Englishmen.

Jim stayed on the raft while the three of us went back to town. Before I knowed it, we were at the Wilks's house. The King and Duke were playing Harvey and William and calling me their servant.

The Wilks girls welcomed us. The oldest was a redhead with the most beautiful face. When the rapscallions said they was her uncles, her eyes lit up. She spread her arms wide. She said her name was Mary Jane and these other two were her sisters.

Mary Jane led us to the parlor. There was a coffin in the room. Well, the King and Duke started crying. You could of heard them clear to New Orleans. I never seen anything so disgusting. It was enough to make a body ashamed of the human race.

Mary Jane said how her father left the girls $6,000.00 in cash. She left the room and came back with a money bag. My, the sight of that money bag got the King's eyes to shining! Before long, Mary Jane was handing the whole bag over to him.

"Dear uncles," she says, "please invest this for me and my sisters."

Later, when they was alone, I saw the King slap the Duke on the back. "This is *bully*!" he says. "It sure beats the Nonesuch, don't it?"

That night they all had a big supper. I stood behind the King and the Duke and waited on them. The two went on and on about their life in England. They was telling stories and making up lies. And the sweet Wilks girls was believing them all.

After dinner, Mary Jane showed us where to sleep. The King and the Duke had one room. It was plain, but nice. I had a little cubbyhole near by.

Well, I couldn't sleep a bit. I sat there thinking how sweet and beautiful that Mary Jane was. I says to myself, I'm *letting* her get robbed of her money. I felt so lowdown and mean! Then I made up my mind. I'd get that money back for her or bust trying.

The next morning, I sneaked into the scoundrels' room. I pawed around a bit. Sure enough, there was the money bag hid under the bed! I had it out fast.

I planned to hide the money somewhere else. And I'd write a note to Mary Jane, telling her where to find it. Then I would hightail it out of there.

That night I waited 'til I heard the Duke and the King snoring. I took the bag of money and slipped downstairs. I was just passing the parlor when I heard someone coming. I ducked into the parlor. The only place I could see to hide the money was in the coffin. So I tucked the money bag under the lid. Then I run and hid behind the door.

The person coming in was Mary Jane. She went to the coffin, kneeled down, and began to cry. She had her back to me, so I slid out of the parlor and went back to my room. I wrote a letter to Mary Jane and left it in her room. It said: *"I put it in the coffin. It was in there when you was crying there in the night. I am mighty sorry for you, Miss Mary Jane."*

I was all set to slip away. Then everything went wrong.

Two more strangers arrived. They said they was the dead man's brothers. Well, these two and the King and the Duke started fighting and arguing. Pretty soon, people began to ask questions. The King and the Duke, they didn't know all that much about Peter Wilks, after all. It was pretty clear that these newcomers was the true brothers. Some folks got real angry. They started calling for ropes and talking about hanging the cheats. I lit out fast as I could.

I had the road all to myself, and I fairly flew. The wind was a-blowing and thunder was crashing all around me.

I found a canoe and paddled out to the raft.

I sprung aboard, yelling, "Get out of the tent, Jim. Set the raft loose! Glory be, we're free of them!"

In two seconds we was sliding down the river. It sure seemed good to be free again and all by ourselves.

Then I looked through the rain, and here they came. The King and the Duke were paddling a canoe as hard as they could. It was all I could do to keep from crying.

"Trying to give us the slip, were you?" says the King as they climbed on board. He grabbed me and shook me by the collar.

I says, "*No*, Your Majesty! It just didn't seem no use for me to stay. I couldn't help you. I didn't want to be hung if I could get away. I feared you and the Duke wasn't alive. I was mighty sorry. So was Jim. We was awful glad to see you coming. Just ask Jim."

Jim said it was so, and the King told him to shut up. Then he shook me again.

Well, after a while, the King settled down. But he was still frightful mad about leaving that money bag behind.

We didn't stop in any town for days. We just

kept moving right down the river. The King and the Duke planned more ways to get money. I could hear them talking in the tent at night. They'd whisper for two or three hours at a time. Jim and me got mighty uneasy. We didn't like the look of it. We were sure they were set to rob somebody's house or store.

One day the King said he was going to town. He said me and the Duke was to come along for him if he wasn't back by noon.

Well, midday came, and no King. So me and the Duke went into town. We hunted around for the King. After a long time, we found him drinking whiskey. The Duke and the King began to argue. The more they argued, the more whiskey they drank. I waited until they was drunk. Then I lit out. I made up my mind that it would be a long day before they ever saw me and Jim again.

I got back to the raft all out of breath. I sung out, "Set her loose, Jim!"

But there weren't no answer. Nobody came out of the tent. Jim was gone!

I went back to shore. For a long time I walked along the road, calling for Jim. Pretty soon I run across a boy. I asked him if he'd seen a stranger. He says he seen an odd fellow leading a slave. He tells me this fellow sold the slave up at the Phelps place for $40.00!

Well, I knew it was Jim. And I knew that the King had sold him away. I went back to the raft, and sat down in the tent. Then I cried. I couldn't help it. After our long journey, it had all come to nothing. After everything we had done for them, those scoundrels had made Jim a slave again for all his life! And they had done that terrible thing for 40 dirty dollars!

I knew what I had to do. I had to steal Jim back. It might be wrong—but all I could picture was Jim before me. He was floating along, singing, talking, and laughing. "All right then, I'll go to hell!" I says aloud. And I set out to steal Jim out of slavery.

| 8 |

I Have a
New Name

I asked around and found the way to the
Phelps place. When I got there, the day was all
quiet and hot and bright. The Phelpses had a little
cotton plantation. There was a main house and a
few log cabins. One little hut stood away off by
the back fence. Some old hounds were sleeping
in the yard.

I went around to the back door of the main
house. I didn't have a plan. I trusted the right
words would come out of my mouth when I
needed them. They usually did.

When I got to the door, the hounds started
a-barking. Then here came a woman running out
the kitchen door. She was about 45 or 50. She
was smiling all over. "It's you, at last!" she says.

She grabbed me and hugged me tight.

"I'm so glad to see you," she cries. "We've been looking for you every time the ferry comes in. Come here, boy—give your Aunt Sally a big hug!"

I was getting uneasy. I guessed this was Mrs. Phelps. Now I had to find out who she thought *I* was. Lucky for me, it wasn't long before she gave it away.

"Your Uncle Silas has just gone to town to fetch you," she says. "You must have missed him on the road. Children, come here!" she calls to the house. "Come out and meet your cousin, Tom Sawyer!"

By jings, I almost fell to the ground! It was like being born again, I was so glad to find out who I was. Now I could answer every question they asked. I told them all about the Sawyer family—about Sid and Aunt Polly and the rest of the clan.

I stayed happy 'til by and by I heard a steamboat coughing along down the river. Then I says to myself, suppose Tom Sawyer is on that boat? What if he comes and sings out my name before I can stop him?

Well, I couldn't have that! I had to go up

the road and catch him. I told Aunt Sally I had to go back to the ferry dock and fetch my baggage.

"Wait for your Uncle Silas to come back with the wagon," she says.

But I says, "No, ma'am. I don't want to bc no trouble. I'll just go myself."

Sure enough, I was just about halfway to the dock when I saw Tom Sawyer coming along the road. He saw me, too. His eyes popped and his mouth dropped open.

"Don't hurt me!" Tom cries out. "You must be Huck Finn's ghost! Why did you come back to haunt me?"

I says, "I ain't come back, Tom! Why, I ain't never been gone!"

"Weren't you ever murdered at all?" asks Tom. His face was still white and scared looking.

"No, I weren't never murdered at all! I just played a trick on Pap. Here, touch me if you don't believe it."

So he touched me, and it satisfied him. And was he ever glad to see me again! He wanted me to tell him every little bit of my grand adventure

I told Tom the whole story. "And there's old Miss Watson's Jim here. I'm a-trying to steal him out of slavery!"

"*What!*" says Tom. "Why, Jim is—"

He stopped and thought a minute.

"I know you think it's a lowdown thing to do," I says. "But I *am* lowdown, and I'm a-going to steal him. You got to keep quiet and not let on, Tom. Will you?"

Then Tom's eyes lit up. He says, "I'll *help* you steal him!"

Well, I was surprised at that! Tom Sawyer was a boy that was respectable and well brought up. Now he was going to help me steal a slave! I couldn't understand it.

We headed back to the Phelps plantation. Along the way we made our plan. I would still play Tom Sawyer. Tom would say he was his brother Sid, come to visit too.

Well, Aunt Sally hugged him and kissed him right away. "What a surprise you are, Sid!" she says. "We weren't looking for you at all, but only Tom."

Tom took right up pretending to be Sid.

"I begged and begged to come, too," says he. "Finally, Aunt Polly let me."

That night, Tom and me was to sleep in the same room. We went up to bed right after supper. But instead of getting to bed, we went out looking for Jim. We climbed out the window and slid down the lightning rod. For a while we roamed around the plantation, but we couldn't find nothing. I guess we was needing an adventure real bad, because we headed for town.

On the road, I told Tom all about life on the raft. I told him about the Duke and the King. But just as I was a-telling him the rest of it, we heard an awful noise. Coming towards us from town was a raging bunch of people. They was carrying torches and whooping and yelling. We jumped to one side to let them go by.

As they passed, I saw what they was doing. They had two fellows riding on a rail. It was the King and the Duke! I hardly knew the two rapscallions. They was covered all over with tar and feathers. They didn't look like nothing that was human.

Well, even though they'd done bad to me and Jim, it made me sick to see it. I was sorry for them two pitiful rascals. That was a dreadful sight to see. Human beings can be awful cruel to each other!

There was nothing we could do. It was too late. We stopped some people on the edge of the crowd and asked them what happened. They said that the rascals put on a terrible show and cheated people out of their money. The whole audience rose up and went for them.

Tom and I poked along back home. I knew I

hadn't done nothing, but I was feeling to blame, somehow.

By and by Tom says, "Looky here, Huck. I bet I know where Jim is. I'll bet he's locked in that old hut by the back fence. I saw a slave taking food down there earlier tonight. He unlocked the door when he took the food in. Then he locked it again when he came out. I saw him handing Uncle Silas the key at dinner time."

I knowed Tom was right! *What a head he had!* If I had Tom Sawyer's head, I wouldn't trade it for nothing!

"Now we got to come up with a plan to steal Jim," says Tom. "I've got an idea! You think up a plan, and I'll think up a plan. Then we'll take the one we like best!"

I went to thinking out a plan, but only just to be doing something. I knew very well where the best plan was going to come from.

| 9 |
Trying to
Help Jim

"Have you got a plan yet?" Tom asks me.

"My plan is this," I says. "First we find out if it's really Jim in the hut. That's easy enough. Then tomorrow night we get my canoe. We go fetch my raft over from the island. Then we wait for a real dark night. We steal the key to the hut and set Jim free. We shove off down the river on the raft. We'll hide daytimes and run nighttimes, the way Jim and I used to do it. How about it, Tom? Wouldn't that plan work?"

"Work? Well, sure it would work. But it's too blame *simple*! What's the good of a plan that ain't nothing more than that?"

Then Tom told me his plan. I saw in a minute that it had more style. Tom's plan would make

Jim a free man and give us some adventure besides!

I won't bother telling the whole plan here. I knowed it wouldn't stay the same, anyway. It would be changing as we went along.

When me and Tom got back to the Phelps plantation, we went straight to the hut. I pointed to a loose board on the outside wall. "We could pull that board right off," I says. "The hole would be big enough for Jim to crawl through."

"Well, I should hope we could find a more exciting plan than *that*, Huck Finn!" says Tom. He looked exasperated.

"Well, then," says I, "how would it be to *saw* him out? That's how I got out of Pap's shed that time."

"That's more like it," says Tom. "That's real mysterious and good. Say! I know what we'll do—we'll *dig* him out."

We found an old pick leaning against the hut. Tom seemed kind of disappointed. I think he'd hoped we'd have to dig under the hut with our hands. We dug and dug with that old pick. After an hour or two, we had a tunnel into the hut.

Jim was there, sure enough. When he saw the

two of us, he sang out with happiness.

"Glory be, it's Huck! And good Lord, ain't that Mister Tom?"

"Yes, it's us! We're going to set you free, Jim," says Tom.

Jim was chained to the iron bed he sat on. "If we can just lift the bed, we can slip off that chain, and make for the raft," says I.

But Tom acted like he never heard me. He shook his head and fell to thinking for a while. Then pretty soon he sighed and shook his head again.

"Well, I guess we don't need to do that after all," he says.

"Do what?" I asks.

"Saw his leg off."

"Good land!" I says. "What would you want to saw his leg off for, anyway?"

"Well," says Tom, "I guess we could sneak Jim a file and a rope ladder made from sheets. People that is escaping always need a rope ladder!"

"Well, if he's got to have it, let him have it," I says. "Let's just get on with it!"

We talked to Jim some more that night.

We promised that we'd get him free soon and tried to cheer him up. Then we went back to our beds.

The next night we slid down the lightning rod again. We had a bag full of stuff that Tom said we'd need. We had candles and bed sheets and an old brass candlestick. We even had a white shirt. Tom said Jim could write the story of his escape on it in blood.

Tom said this was the most fun he'd had in ages. And just to keep the plan from going off too easy and boring, he added another fine touch. He wrote a letter and left it in the kitchen. The letter said:

"A desperate gang of cutthroats is going to steal the runaway slave tonight. Signed, An Unknown Friend."

Well, Tom's letter sure got him plenty of excitement. By the time we got Jim out of the hut, 15 farmers with guns was hiding around the yard!

Lucky it was a dark night. We slipped out the tunnel. Not making the least noise, we creeped to the fence. Me and Jim got over the fence all right. But Tom's britches catched fast on a splinter on the top rail. When he pulled loose, he made a little noise.

"Who's that?" a man's voice sings out. "Answer or I'll shoot!"

We didn't answer. Then we heard a *bang, bang, bang!* Bullets whizzed around us! We ran as fast as we could for the river.

We got to the canoe and hopped in. Then we struck out for the island where my raft was. Pretty soon the sounds of guns and yelling got dim and died out.

When we stepped onto my old raft at last, I says, "Now, old Jim, you're a free man again. And you ain't never going to be a slave no more!"

"That was a mighty fine plan!" says Jim.

We was all glad as we could be. Tom was the gladdest of all. He said this was an honest adventure because this time he had a real bullet in his leg.

When me and Jim heard that, we wasn't so happy after all. The bullethole was hurting Tom, and it was starting to bleed pretty bad. We laid him in the tent and tore up the white shirt to use as a bandage.

Tom grabbed the cloth away. "I can do it

myself," he says. "Let's shove off!"

But me and Jim got to thinking and talking. "I don't move another step without a doctor for that leg," says I.

Tom made a fuss, but me and Jim wouldn't give in. I struck out for town in the canoe. The plan was for Jim to hide in the woods when he saw the doctor coming.

I woke up the doctor in town. He was a nice, kind-looking man. I told him me and my brother was out hunting yesterday and had camped on an old raft we found. I said my brother shot himself by accident and needed help.

"Who's your folks?" the doctor asks.

"The Phelpses, down yonder," I says.

"Oh," says he.

After a minute he lit up his lantern and got his bag. We started out. But he said my canoe didn't look strong enough to carry two people. He said for me to wait right there until he come back. Then he took my canoe and shoved off.

I laid down by a lumber pile to wait. Next thing I knew I was waking up and the sun was high. I jumped up. But before I could move, here came Uncle Silas walking around the corner.

"Tom Sawyer! Where have you been, you rascal?" he says. "Your aunt's been mighty worried about you."

"Me and Sid have been hunting that slave who ran away. Sid's over at the post office waiting to see if there's any news. I was just going to get us something to eat."

Uncle Silas led me to the post office to get Sid. Just as I knew, he wasn't there.

"Come along home," says Uncle Silas. "Sid will show up sooner or later."

I knew it weren't no use arguing, so I went along with him.

Back at the house, Aunt Sally was glad to see me. She laughed and cried and hugged me. Then we waited and waited for Sid to show up.

"What could have become of that boy?" says Aunt Sally. I could see that she was mighty uneasy.

"I'll run to town and get him," I says.

"Oh, no, you won't!" says she. "One lost boy is enough!"

"Boys will be boys," says Uncle Silas. "Sid will turn up in the morning."

Aunt Sally said she'd sit up looking for him

a while. She kept a light burning so he would see it. She kept checking on me and hugging me. When I got up in the night, I saw Aunt Sally sitting by her candle. Her eyes were looking out toward the road. She was crying. That made me feel mean.

It was dawn when I waked up again. Aunt Sally was sitting there yet—her candle almost out. Her gray head was resting on her hand. She was asleep.

| 10 |

Why They
Don't Hang Jim

Uncle Silas went to town and back again before breakfast. He told Aunt Sally that there weren't no sight of Sid anywhere. Then the two of them sat at the breakfast table, looking sad and worried.

By and by Uncle Silas says, "Did I give you that letter?"

"What letter?" says Aunt Sally.

"The one I got yesterday out of the post office," he says. He looked through his pockets. Then he handed it to her.

"Why, it's from Sis."

I was thinking there'd be trouble now. But before Aunt Sally could open the letter, she dropped it. She jumped up because she saw something moving outside the window.

And so did I.

It was Tom Sawyer! A bunch of men were carrying him on a mattress. There was that old doctor. And there was Jim, with his hands tied behind him.

Aunt Sally ran outside.

I hid the letter behind the first thing I saw. Then I ran outdoors, too.

Aunt Sally flung herself at Tom.

"Oh, the poor boy's dead. I just know he's dead!" she cries out.

Tom turned his head a little. He muttered something that didn't make sense.

Aunt Sally flung up her hands. "He's alive! Thank God!" She kissed him. Then she ran to get his bed ready.

Uncle Silas and the doctor followed after Tom into the house. I followed after the men. I had to see what they was going to do with poor old Jim.

The men was awful mad. Some of them wanted to hang Jim for running away. They swore at him and slapped him in the head every once in a while. Jim never said nothing. He never let on that he knew me.

They took him to the same hut. They chained him up good this time. They chained his hands and both legs, too. They said he wasn't to have nothing to eat but bread and water. They said a couple of farmers with guns would guard the hut day and night.

Then the old doctor came in the hut. He took a look. Then he says, "Don't be too rough on him. He ain't a bad fellow. When I got to the boy, I saw that I couldn't cut the bullet out without help. I yelled out loud, 'I got to have help!' Well, out crawls this slave from somewheres. He says that he'll help. He did a good job, too. And he risked his freedom to do it."

The old doctor went on with his story. "Well, there I was with the two of them. I didn't know what I'd do next. Then some men in a skiff came by. They grabbed the runaway. Before he knowed what was happening, they tied him up good. We never had no trouble with him. He ain't so bad, gentlemen. That's what I think about him."

After hearing the doctor's story, the men softened up a little. I was mighty thankful to that old doctor. I knew I'd judged him right. He was a good man with a good heart. They all agreed that Jim had acted honorable. Every one of those men promised that they wouldn't swear at him no more. I hoped they'd say he didn't have to have all those heavy chains on. But they didn't think of it. I thought it was best for me to keep still.

Next morning I heard that Tom was better. Aunt Sally had gone to take a nap, so I slipped into the sickroom. Tom was sleeping very peaceful. I sat down and waited for him to wake up.

Pretty soon Aunt Sally came in and sat down beside me. We sat there watching.

By and by, Tom waked up. He took a look around. Then he says, "Hello! Why, I'm home! Where's the raft?"

"It's all right," I says.

"What about Jim?"

"The same," I says kind of quiet. I didn't want to say too much.

But Tom goes on. "Good! Now we're all safe. Did you tell Aunty?"

"About what, Sid?" asks Aunt Sally.

"Why, the whole thing—how we set the runaway slave free."

"Oh, dear!" cries Aunt Sally. "The poor child is out of his head again."

"No, I ain't," says Tom. "We did set him free. We laid out a plan, and we done it."

Then Tom told Aunt Sally the whole darned story. I could see that it weren't no use trying to stop him.

"Why Aunty, it was a fine plan—and a lot of work. We had to steal candles and bed sheets and stuff. We used the canoe to get out to the raft. Then we were safe and Jim was a free man. We done it all by ourselves—and it was great fun, too!"

"Well, I never heard the likes of it!" says Aunt Sally. "You scared us half to death. Why, if I ever catch you meddling with the likes of him again—"

"Meddling with who, Aunty?" asks Tom.

"Why, I'm talking about the runaway slave, of course."

Tom got very serious then. He looks at me and says, "Didn't you tell me he was all right? Didn't Jim get away?"

"Indeed, he *didn't* get away!" says Aunt Sally. "They captured him and put him in the hut again. He's loaded down with chains until he's claimed or sold!"

Tom rose up in bed. His eyes flashed. "They got *no right* to lock him up!" he cries. "Turn him loose! He ain't no slave. He's as free as any creature that walks this earth!"

"What can you mean, child?"

"I mean every word I say, Aunt Sally! Old Miss Watson died two months ago. She was sorry she ever even thought about selling him down the river. She said so—and she set him free in her will!"

"If he was already free, what on earth did you want to set him free for?"

"Why, I wanted the adventure of it!" says Tom. "I just wanted to have some—" Tom stopped and stared at the door. "Goodness alive, it's Aunt Polly!" he says.

There she was, standing in the door.

Aunt Sally jumped for her. The two sisters hugged and cried. I took the chance to hide under the bed.

"Tom, what have you gotten yourself into now?" Aunt Polly says.

"Why, that ain't Tom!" says Aunt Sally. "It's Sid! Tom is—Tom? Tom? Why, where is Tom? He was here a minute ago."

"You mean Huck Finn? I see him right there. Come out from under that bed, Huck Finn," says Aunt Polly.

So I done it. Aunt Sally, she looked pretty mixed up for a while. Then Tom's Aunt Polly told all about who I was. I had to up and tell the truth. I told how Mrs. Phelps had taken me for Tom Sawyer.

"Oh, Huck—you can go ahead and call me Aunt Sally," she says. "I'm used to it now."

Aunt Polly said that Tom was right. It was a fact that old Miss Watson had set Jim free in her will. Sure enough, Tom Sawyer and I had gone to all that trouble to free somebody that was already free!

"I got a letter saying Sid was here," Aunt Polly says. "That's when I knew something was up. Why, Sally, I wrote you two letters asking what you could mean."

"Well, I never heard *nothing* from you!" says Aunt Sally. "What could have happened to those letters?"

Then both the aunts turned and looked at me and Tom.

We saw it was best to say nothing.

| 11 |
Nothing More
to Write

The first time I got Tom alone, I asked him to explain what he had been thinking. Why had we worked so hard to free a man who was *already* free?

He said he'd planned it in his head from the start. He wanted us to run down the river on the raft so we'd have some adventures. Then we'd tell Jim about Miss Watson setting him free. To celebrate, we'd take him home on a steamboat in style. We'd pay him for his lost time, too. Jim would have been a hero—and so would we!

That all sounded pretty good. But I reckoned it ended up pretty good just the way it was.

Because of what the doctor said, the men let Jim out of those heavy chains. Then Aunt Polly,

Uncle Silas, and Aunt Sally heard how Jim helped the doctor care for Tom. They made a big fuss over old Jim. After eating all he wanted, he came up to the sickroom to visit Tom. We all had a good long talk. Then Tom gave Jim $40.00 for being a prisoner and doing it so good!

Tom talked on and on. "Let's all three of us slide out of here one of these nights," he says. "We'll buy supplies. Then we'll go out on some howling adventures for a week or two."

I said that sounded fine, but I didn't have money for supplies. "It's likely that Pap's been back. By now he'll have gotten all my money away from Judge Thatcher."

"No, Huck, the money's still there," says Tom. "All $6,000.00 of it. Your Pap ain't been back at all. At least he hadn't showed up before I left town."

Then Jim speaks up kind of serious. "He ain't coming back no more, Huck."

I says, "Why, Jim? How do you know?"

"Never mind that, Huck. He just ain't coming back."

But I kept at him.

At last Jim says, "Do you remember the

house we found floating down the river? There was a dead man in there, and I didn't let you see him. Well, you can get your money when you want it. That man was your Pap."

* * * *

Tom is almost well now. He's got the bullet that was in his leg on a watch chain. He wears it around his neck.

I guess there ain't nothing more to write about, and I'm glad of it. If I'd knowed what trouble it was to write a book, I wouldn't have tried it. I ain't going to no more!

I reckon I got to take the raft out now. I want to slip out of here ahead of the rest. Aunt Sally took a notion that *she* wants to adopt me and civilize me now. I knowed I couldn't stand that. I been there before.

Activities
The Adventures of Huckleberry Finn

BOOK SEQUENCE
First complete the sentences with words from the box. Then number the events to show which happened first, second, and so on.

lazy	britches	berries	worth	fog
dock	bandage	coffin	cowards	hat
trash	feathers	robber	prisoner	

_____ 1. Huck says the Shepherdsons must be _____.

_____ 2. Tom hangs Jim's _____ in a tree.

_____ 3. Huck goes to the _____ to meet Tom Sawyer.

_____ 4. Jim brags that he's _____ $800.

_____ 5. Huck soon gets used to the _____ life.

_____ 6. The rapscallions are covered with tar and _____.

_____ 7. Huck hides the moneybag in the _____.

_____ 8. Huck and Jim tear up a white sheet to make a _____ for Tom.

_____ 9. Huck wants to join Tom's _____ gang.

_____ 10. Tom gives Jim $40 for being such a good _____.

_____ 11. Jim says that people who make a fool of a friend are _____.

_____ 12. When he first sees the rapscallions, Huck is out looking for _____.

_____ 13. Tom's _____ get caught by a splinter on the fence.

_____ 14. In the _____, the raft passes right by Cairo.

FACTS ABOUT CHARACTERS

Reread Chapter 1 and answer below.

A. Circle two words that describe each character.

1. **Pap**   ragged   caring   drunk   worried

2. **Jim**   educated   delicate   superstitious   sleepy

3. **Miss Watson**   scolding   tender   playful   religious

4. **Tom Sawyer**   elderly   imaginative
                   unpopular   adventurous

5. **Huck Finn**   uncivilized   cruel   wealthy   young

B. Complete each sentence with a character's name from the box below.

Widow Douglas	**Mark Twain**	**Huck Finn**	**Jim**
Judge Thatcher	**Miss Watson**	**Tom Sawyer**	**Pap**

1. _____ handed out a dollar a day to Tom and Huck.

2. _____ hadn't seen his son for more than a year.

3. _____ took Huck in to live with her.

4. _____ was the first captain of the robber band.

5. _____ thought some witches left him a five-cent piece.

6. _____ sometimes said that Huck was wicked.

7. _____ said he doesn't
like stories about dead people.

8. _____ introduced Huck
in *The Adventures of Tom Sawyer*.

CAUSE AND EFFECT 1
Reread Chapter 5 and answer below.

A. Write the letter to match each *cause* on the left with
its *effect* on the right.

CAUSE

1. ___ Huck wants
people to think
he's been killed.

2. ___ Huck says that his
family has died.

3. ___ Jim is waiting for
Huck in the swamp.

4. ___ Sophia runs
off with Harney
Shepherdson.

5. ___ Buck is killed.

EFFECT

a. The Grangerfords
take him in.

b. Huck cries a little.

c. The Grangerfords
go for their guns.

d. He makes up a
new name.

e. Jack says he
wants to show
Huck something.

B. Circle a letter to show the *cause* of each
boldfaced *effect* described below.

1. **Huck tricks Buck into spelling his name.**

a. Huck forgot the name.

b. Huck wanted to play a joke.

2. **The Grangerfords are in a feud with the Shepherdsons.**

   a. A Grangerford insulted a Shepherdson.

   b. Some unexplained trouble started 30 years ago.

3. **Jim is afraid to call out to Huck.**

   a. He is frightened of slave-catchers.

   b. He knows Huck can't hear him.

4. **Huck won't describe the fight he saw.**

   a. He couldn't see it very well.

   b. It would make him sick to tell it.

COMPREHENSION CHECK

Reread Chapter 8. Then circle a letter to show the correct answer to each question.

1. What was strange about the greeting Huck got at the Phelps place?

   a. Huck didn't expect the hounds to bark.

   b. Mrs. Phelps thought he was Tom Sawyer.

   c. Aunt Sally was smiling all over.

   d. Huck had missed Uncle Silas on the road.

2. Why did the sound of a steamboat suddenly make Huck worried?

   a. The steamboat could explode.

   b. It reminded Huck of Jim.

   c. He wanted to stay with Aunt Sally.

   d. Tom might be on that boat.

3. Why was Tom Sawyer's face "white and scared-looking"?

   a. He thought Huck's ghost was haunting him.

   b. He was so happy to see Huck again.

   c. The boat trip had made him seasick.

   d. Uncle Silas had not come to fetch him.

4. What did Huck and Tom tell the Phelps family?

   a. They complained about being sent to bed.

   b. They said that Aunt Polly was coming soon.

   c. They said that Tom was his brother, Sid.

   d. They asked to go into town that night.

5. How did Huck feel when he saw what happened to the King and the Duke?

   a. He was afraid the crowd would attack him next.

   b. He was glad they finally got caught.

   c. He and Tom started to laugh.

   d. He felt sorry for the pitiful rascals.

CAUSE AND EFFECT 2

Reread Chapter 11. Notice that each sentence begins with a *cause*. Look in the box for the *effect* of each *cause*, and use it to complete the sentence.

> •**he decides to slip away on his raft.**
> •**he made a fine plan to set Jim free.**
> •**he tells Huck that Pap isn't coming back.**
> •**they make a big fuss over him.**
> •**the men take off his heavy chains.**
> •**he says he can't afford to buy supplies.**

1. Jim sees Pap's body in the floating house, so _____

   _____

2. Aunt Sally wants to civilize Huck, so _____

   _____

3. Tom wanted some adventures, so _____

   _____

4. Aunt Polly and the Phelpses hear how Jim helped Tom, so _____

   _____

5. Huck thinks Pap probably has his money, so _____

   _____

6. The doctor told everyone that Jim was a good man, so _____

   _____

FINAL EXAM

Circle a letter to show how each sentence should be completed.

1. **Huck and Tom got rich**
   a. from the profits of Mark Twain's book.
   b. by inheriting money from Miss Watson.
   c. by discovering robber's gold hidden in a cave.
   d. by working for a dollar a day, all year round.

2. **Huck stayed with the Widow Douglas because**
   a. Judge Thatcher ordered him to go there.
   b. he hadn't seen his father in a year.
   c. the Finns' house had recently burned down.
   d. there was no room at Tom Sawyer's

3. **Jim thought Huck was a ghost because**
   a. he had heard that Huck had been murdered.
   b. Huck's face was very pale.
   c. Huck often visited the cemetery.
   d. Jim saw ghosts all around him.

4. **Huck told the woman in the shack**
   a. that he and Jim were running away.
   b. never to touch a snakeskin.
   c. that a reward was out for him and Pap.
   d. that he ran away from a mean old farmer.

5. **When Huck told the slave-catchers his family was sick**
   a. they insisted on coming aboard to see for themselves.
   b. they knew he was telling a lie.
   c. they gave him two $20 gold pieces.
   d. they asked which way Jim went.

6. **In a free state Jim could save money to**
   a. buy his wife and children from their masters.
   b. get a nice raft of his own.
   c. sue Miss Watson for scaring him so badly.
   d. take a wonderful long vacation.

Answers to Activities
The Adventures of Huckleberry Finn

BOOK SEQUENCE
1. 7/cowards   2. 2/hat   3. 10/dock   4. 4/worth
5. 3/lazy   6. 11/feathers   7. 9/coffin   8. 13/bandage
9. 1/robber   10. 14/prisoner   11. 5/trash
12. 8/berries   13. 12/britches   14. 6/fog

FACTS ABOUT CHARACTERS
A. 1. ragged, drunk   2. superstitious, sleepy
   3. scolding, religious   4. imaginative, adventurous
   5. uncivilized, young
B. 1. Judge Thatcher   2. Pap   3. Widow Douglas
   4. Tom Sawyer   5. Jim   6. Miss Watson
   7. Huck Finn   8. Mark Twain

CAUSE AND EFFECT 1
A. 1. d   2. a   3. e   4. c   5. b
B. 1. a   2. b   3. a   4. b

COMPREHENSION CHECK
1. b   2. d   3. a   4. c   5. d

CAUSE AND EFFECT 2
1. he tells Huck that Pap isn't coming back
2. he decides to slip away on his raft
3. he made a fine plan to set Jim free
4. they make a big fuss over him
5. he says he can't afford to buy supplies
6. the men take off his heavy chains

FINAL EXAM
1. c   2. b   3. a   4. d   5. c   6. a